# Jack and the Hungry Bear

Published in 2013 by Wayland

Wayland
338 Euston Road
London NW1 3BH

Wayland Australia
Level 17/207 Kent Street
Sydney, NSW 2000

The rights of Andy Blackford to be identified as the Author and
Marijke Van Veldhoven to be identified as the Illustrator of this Work have been
asserted by them in accordance with the Copyright, Designs and Patents Act, 1988.

All rights reserved

Series Editor: Louise John
Cover design: Paul Cherrill
Design: D.R.ink
Consultant: Shirley Bickler

A CIP catalogue record for this book is available from the British Library.

ISBN 9780750259606

Printed in China

This edition first published in 2010 by Wayland
Reprinted in 2011 and 2013

Text copyright © Andy Blackford 2009
Illustration copyright © Marijke Van Veldhoven 2009

Wayland is a division of Hachette Children's Books,
an Hachette UK Company

www.hachette.co.uk

# Jack and the Hungry Bear

Written by Andy Blackford
Illustrated by Marijke Van Veldhoven

WAYLAND

Jack was watching TV.
The film was about some
cheeky bears in America.

"The bears climb into people's gardens and tip their dustbins over. They hunt for food and make lots of mess," said the man on the TV.

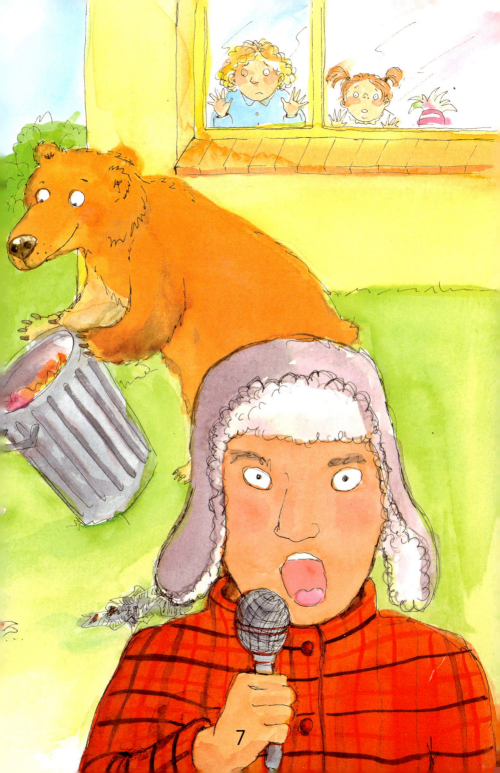

Next day, Jack looked out of his window. The bin bags were torn open and there was rubbish all over the grass.

Jack's dad was very cross. "Who would do a thing like that?"

"Foxes, maybe," said Mum.

"A hungry bear!" said Jack.

"We live in England, Jack," said his dad. "There are no bears in England."

But Dad was wrong. There was one in the wood shed. A very big one.

She was fast asleep, and she was snoring very loudly.

"Dad," said Jack. "There's a bear in the wood shed!"

"Oh, Jack," smiled Dad. "Run along and play now."

Jack went back to the shed. "HELLO!" he shouted in the bear's ear.

The bear woke up. "You made me jump!" she grumbled.

"Sorry," said Jack. "But I wanted to ask, why are you sleeping in our shed?"

"I'm sorry," said the bear.
"But I missed the last bus
home to the zoo."

"I didn't know bears went on buses," said Jack.

"We do on Fridays," the bear said. "That's when we do our shopping."

"I was so busy shopping that I forgot the time," said the bear. "When I got to the bus stop, the bus had already gone."

"I smelled your old bin bags and I found some chicken leftovers inside. A bit old, but they were still tasty."

"OK, but you'll have to clean up this mess. There's rubbish everywhere!"

"Ah yes, of course!" replied the bear. So she did.

Jack's mum gave her a sticky bun and a cup of tea. Then Jack's dad drove her back to the zoo.

"Do you want to come for tea on Friday?" asked Jack. "We're having chicken!"

"Great!" replied the bear.
"Can we eat it in
the garden?"

"As long as you don't make a mess on the grass again!" Jack laughed.

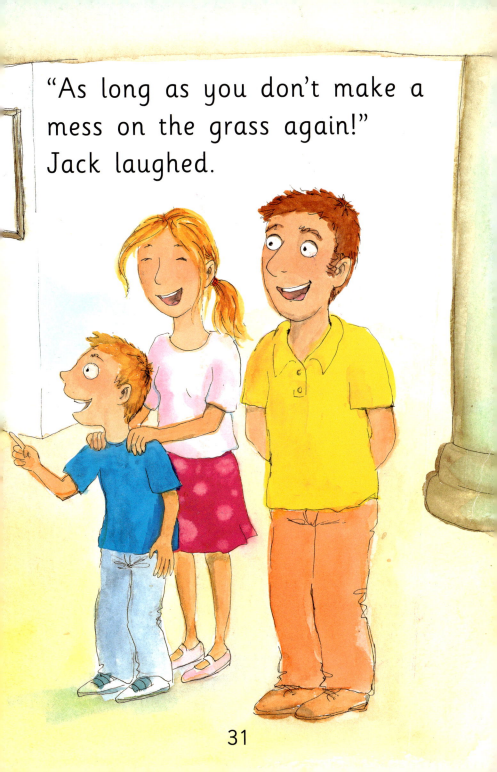

**START READING** is a series of highly enjoyable books for beginner readers. **The books have been carefully graded to match the Book Bands widely used in schools.** This enables readers to be sure they choose books that match their own reading ability.

**Look out for the Band colour on the book in our Start Reading logo.**

The Bands are:

- Pink Band 1
- Red Band 2
- Yellow Band 3
- Blue Band 4
- Green Band 5
- Orange Band 6
- Turquoise Band 7
- Purple Band 8
- Gold Band 9

**START READING** books can be read independently or shared with an adult. They promote the enjoyment of reading through satisfying stories supported by fun illustrations.

**Andy Blackford** used to play guitar in a rock band. Besides books, he writes about running and scuba diving. He has run across the Sahara Desert and dived with tiger sharks. He lives in the country with his wife and daughter, a friendly collie dog and a grumpy cat.

**Marijke Van Veldhoven** loves to make people laugh. At school she liked drawing cartoons of her friends and teachers that had everyone in hysterics! She lives happily in the Netherlands with her dog and two cats and enjoys long walks.